THE PROMISE

A STARLITE MYSTERY

THE STARLITE SUPERNATURAL MYSTERY SERIES

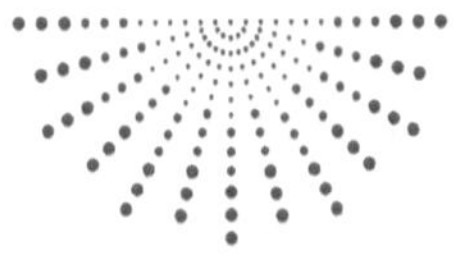

RAY & MICHELE FRASER

Hidden Door Press
Los Angeles, CA

Proofread by Paula Bothwell
www.pbproofreads.com

Cover design by Michele Fraser

~

We dedicate this story to Ray's best friend, Marine Sergeant Fred Kansik. An American hero who selflessly sacrificed his life in service to our country during the Vietnam War.

~

CHAPTER ONE

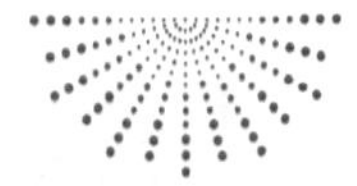

"Emily? Emily? Can you hear me? If you can hear me, say something so that I can find you. Emily? Please say something."

Timmy stayed silent for a few moments, knowing that sound doesn't travel well in the ethers between worlds.

"Emily, if you can hear me, say something," he tried again.

Silence.

I know she's here; he thought. I can feel her energy.

Timmy took a deep breath and shouted as loud as he could, "Emily," dragging the name out into three syllables.

"Daddy?" the soft tinny voice whispered in the stillness. "Is that you, Daddy?"

Timmy rushed to the place where the voice had originated. In the cloudy, dark fog that exists between the physical and spiritual worlds, Timmy could see the small figure standing just before him. He walked to where she stood.

"Emily?" he whispered.

The little girl nodded. She appeared to be four or five years old. Her blonde hair was tousled, in need of a good brushing. She looked totally frustrated and confused.

"No, I'm not your daddy," Timmy answered, "but I'm here to help you. I know where he is."

"Will you take me to him?" she asked.

"Yes. We're going to see your daddy, mommy, and Trent. They've all been waiting for you for a long time. Take my hand and I'll take you to them."

"Why can't my daddy come for me?"

Timmy reached down and felt Emily's small hand join his.

"Because not everyone can see well in the dark. That's why I'm here. I'm going to help you into the light. Then you'll be with your family."

Timmy closed his eyes and sensed the power of the light. After a moment of reflection, he began walking. Emily came with him, keeping step by his side.

"Now, in only a couple of minutes, you'll be home," he said.

Off in the distance, the shimmer of a brilliant light could be seen glowing in the darkness.

"Mister, is that the light?"

"Yes, it is."

"Goodie," Emily exclaimed, drawing the word out. "I never thought I would find my way."

Timmy smiled. "It's okay. Now, your mom and dad can stop worrying and you can all get on with being a family again."

The light grew brighter and brighter with each step.

Despite its brilliance, there was no discomfort in their eyes. After what seemed to be another minute of walking, they stood at the end of the radiant tunnel of white light that bridges the space between the physical world and our spiritual afterlife.

"Look at the other end of the tunnel, Emily. Look who's waiting for you."

At the other end of the light stood Emily's mother, father, and brother. They had all been killed instantly in the violent car accident that had also taken Emily's life. They appeared relieved and happy to see her.

The small girl looked up at Timmy. "Are you coming with me?"

He shook his head. "No, Emily, I can't enter the light yet. Once you step inside, you'll know what to do. Now, hurry along. Your folks are waiting for you."

Emily looked back at Timmy one last time and then stepped into the light. He stood and watched as Emily ran faster and faster, racing through the tunnel and into the arms of her waiting family. His work was complete. Now he could get some rest. It had been a long night.

CHAPTER TWO

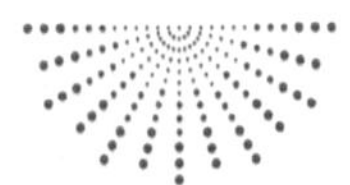

"Tim? I know you can hear me. Why don't you answer? It won't do you any good to ignore me."

Timmy Baker pulled the covers more tightly over his head and closed his eyes.

"Please, please, just go away. You're not real. My mom says you're not real," he whispered.

The soft female voice laughed.

"Tim, you know that we're real. Even your mom knows it. She just doesn't want you to be afraid. Have we done anything to frighten you?"

Yes, he was very frightened. Almost every night for the last two weeks, the voices had come. It was always the same. At 2:22 in the morning, they would call his name. It was always the lady first, and when he didn't answer, the man would come in and call him.

Timmy was eleven years old. His mom had told him he

was special and that maybe he had a gift. All he knew was that he was tired and wanted to rest.

For a while, Timmy had let his dog Buddy sleep at the foot of his bed. On those nights, the voices seldom called. Sadly, one night, they startled Buddy, who began barking loudly. Timmy's dad thought Buddy had to go outside to use the bathroom. After that, Buddy wasn't allowed in his room at night.

He was nervous to talk to his dad about the voices. Carl Baker was a rigid man. In his eyes, boys weren't fearful of anything. Timmy's mom said his dad was like that because he had been frightened of so many things when he was a boy and didn't want his son to be the same way.

When the voices first came, Timmy didn't know what to make of them. He looked all around his bedroom, trying to find out where they were coming from, but the nearest he could figure was they were coming from his closet. That scared him a lot. When he talked to his mother about it, she got a real funny look on her face and didn't say anything for a minute. Then she took a deep breath and told him that the voices weren't real. He thought, *If she was here now, she'd know they were real.*

"Tim, we won't hurt you, we're actually your friends," the voice said, ending abruptly at the opening of his bedroom door. It was his dad.

"Timmy, who were you talking to?"

He hesitated. "Uh, no one, Dad."

Carl turned on the light and walked around the bedroom. He looked in the closet and then turned to look at his son.

"Are you sure you weren't talking to someone?" he asked.

Timmy mumbled. "I'm sure, Dad."

"Why is your closet so cold?"

"I don't know, but could you leave the bedroom door open? Maybe that will warm it up."

Carl Baker nodded. "Okay, get some sleep. You've got school tomorrow."

Timmy put his head down on the pillow and pulled the covers up under his chin.

"I'll try, Dad. Good night."

"Don't try, son. Do. Remember, Bakers don't try, they do. Now, get some rest."

"Yes, Dad," Timmy whispered, closing his eyes.

He heard his parents' bedroom door close and waited for the voices to return. His room remained quiet. In only a few minutes, he was sound asleep.

"Timmy, time to get up," his mother's voice sang.

"I'm up, Mom," he answered, swinging his legs out of the bed and standing up to stretch.

Timmy was looking forward to going to school because at least he felt safe there. No one would talk to him unless Mrs. Childress let them. She was a strict teacher, but she liked Timmy and he liked her.

Timmy's dad had already left early for work, and since his mother was employed part-time at a bakery, she was always there to see him off to school and was home before he got off the bus. She had cereal and toast waiting when he walked into the kitchen.

Timmy had put on his favorite football shirt—for the

third time this week. His mother looked at him and rolled her eyes.

"You're not wearing that shirt to school again this week. Mrs. Childress will think you don't have any other clothes."

"But, Mom," Timmy whined, drawing out the word mom. "It's my favorite shirt."

"It doesn't matter. Today, you're going to wear another favorite shirt, any shirt but that one. Now, eat your breakfast, and I'll bring you something different."

Timmy's second favorite was his Spiderman shirt. It lay unworn in his dresser drawer. He tried not to choose it too often because he didn't want to wear it out. His football shirt seemed rugged and could withstand all the rough play at gym and recess.

Timmy tugged off the football shirt right before his mom handed him something different. Once it was in place, he finished his breakfast and put on his light jacket. Timmy had just grabbed his lunch box when he heard the school bus horn.

"Bye, Mom," he yelled, running out the door and into the bright sunlight.

"Bye, honey," Rose responded, waving to him as he climbed the steps into the bus.

Rose sighed. Before long, she would need to have a very serious talk with Timmy. Carl was against it, but there was no way they could back out of their agreement. Rose shook her head. They just didn't have a choice.

It was almost time to leave for work. She decided to make Timmy's bed before leaving.

"Rose, we need to talk to you," the female voice said.

Rose ignored the sound and went about spreading the sheets smoothly on Timmy's bed, then pulled up the comforter. When she was done, she turned toward the voice and sat down on the bed. A shadowy, holographic image of a man and a woman stood just inside the door of his bedroom.

"So, talk," she blurted, with a hint of disgust in her tone.

The short bald man spoke, his jowls bouncing as he did.

"Now, Rose. You and Carl both agreed. We're here to be sure the arrangement is carried out as promised."

"And if it isn't?" Rose asked.

"Oh, it will be," the slender woman replied. "One way or the other."

Rose stared at the woman. The rouge was too dark on her high cheekbones, and her lipstick outlined a lip-line that wasn't there. Her eyes were dark and emotionless.

"Why don't you leave him alone? When he's an adult, you can have him do whatever it is you need. He's just a kid, for heaven's sake. Let him grow up."

The stocky, gruff-looking man added, "In your eyes, he's an eleven-year-old boy. He's much more than that to us. As Carrin says, we need him and we shall have him. You and Carl made the deal. You can honor your contract, or we can take matters into our own hands. The choice is yours."

Rose looked into the man's eyes. "I'll talk to Carl when he gets home. We'll be in touch with you. In the meantime, leave Timmy alone. He needs his sleep."

The images of the man and woman shivered like a mirage fading in the sun as they disappeared.

CHAPTER THREE

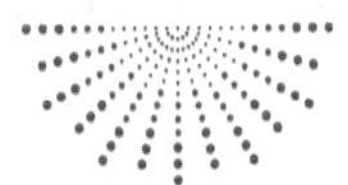

It was eight years ago that Carl and Rose had been confronted with Timmy's destiny in life. The lady in the business suit came to their house two days after his third birthday. She had seemed cordial enough, but there was something about her that seemed out of place. Rose was the first to detect a darker energy in the woman's words.

"I don't like her, Carl. There's something about her that isn't right," Rose had whispered when they went into the kitchen to get coffee for their visitor.

At first, Carl didn't see anything wrong with the lady who said her name was Carrin Atworthy. Her business card showed she was a Director of Inter-dimensional Studies at Fargutt University. Fargutt was a well-known college and one with a strong reputation. What could possibly be wrong with that picture? Carl's first thought was that Rose was simply over-reacting. He was soon to find out either he was losing his mind, or there was a sinister aspect to Ms. Atworthy.

The conversation commenced with the normal pleasantries. They discussed the weather. Summer was near and travel plans were in the future. In short, it started off with the usual topics for any introductory visit. Following her second sip of coffee, the well-dressed lady placed her china cup in the saucer, took a deep breath, and began.

"Mr. and Mrs. Baker, may I call you Rose and Carl?"

After their assent, Ms. Atworthy proceeded in much the same manner as a professor might in presenting a lecture.

"As I mentioned, I'm a director of Inter-dimensional Studies at Fargutt. For the average student, this program is a course of study that allows them to focus on the development and function of our universal systems. It's one that people enjoy because it answers many questions." Carrin paused, took another sip of coffee, and continued, "However, that curriculum is only a front for what our true purpose is."

Carl sensed a chill run through his body and knew that Rose's initial impression of Carrin was accurate.

"And what might the true purpose be?" he pondered.

The look on her face told Carl that he probably wasn't prepared for the answer she was about to give.

Ms. Atworthy glanced briefly at Rose and then returned her gaze to Carl.

"How familiar are you with dimensional issues?" she inquired.

Carl shrugged. "I'm not. I leave it to the intellectuals," he answered. "Stuff like that makes my brain hurt."

Carrin nodded. "Well, today, I'm going to introduce you to a concept that will truly push you to the edge of your understanding. The idea I'm going to present will take a bit of getting used to, but I assure you, it is fact and is part of your future. To use your own terms, this may make your brain hurt."

"What exactly is that supposed to mean?" Rose interjected.

"It means," Carrin stated, "what you see as your world is not really what you believe. Things are a tad more—should I say, *complex*, than what you perceive."

Carl sat up in his chair and placed his coffee cup on the table.

"Complex?" he hollered. "What do you mean, complex?"

Carl's question was the cue their visitor had been waiting for.

"I'm glad you asked me that, Carl. You see, most earth-bound people have a very limited perception of their existence. They believe our essence operates in three dimensions and that life and death factors related to their physical bodies are the only controlling energies that matter. Sadly, they're mistaken."

"What other factors are there?" Rose questioned with trepidation in her voice.

Carrin slowly shook her head. "Oh, Rose. There are way too many to enumerate. You wouldn't be able to understand most of them, anyway. For now, let's focus on the ones that will apply to you and Timmy."

"Timmy?" Carl shouted. "What the hell does any of this have to do with him?"

Carrin got serious. "I anticipated you might have some difficulty in accepting what I'm about to tell you. It's very normal. When people make promises, they tend to forget them as time passes. We've dealt with similar reactions from many of our families. I ask only that you hear me out and take a period of reflection to think about the information before you react."

Neither Carl nor Rose said anything in response, so she continued, "Good. Let's begin."

Carrin told the story of Carl and Rose praying for help in conceiving a child. It appeared that Rose was infertile and having a child would be impossible. Following their beliefs, they prayed, promising to do anything if their wish for a baby was granted. "Your prayers were heard," Carrin exclaimed.

"You see," she continued, "when you promised you would do anything to have a child, it caught the attention of the powers that be. There are things which must be done that earthly people must do."

"Earthly people?" Carl grumbled. "What the hell is that supposed to mean?"

Carrin continued to smile and looked directly at Carl. "Please calm down. This is not at all negative, but you did promise. We're just ensuring that you make good on your commitment."

Carl leaped to his feet. "We made no promises. If you think we did, sue us. Prove it in court. We didn't make any agreement."

Once again, the smile never wavered. "Carl, please sit down. You're only making this more difficult. I asked you to hear me out. Won't you please grant me that courtesy?"

"I want you out of my house," Carl demanded with a wave of his arm toward the front door. "If you have any case against us, file it. If not, leave us alone!"

Carrin sighed deeply and looked toward the door. Before she moved, she spoke directly to Rose.

"You know the promises you made. You said you would do *anything* to have a child. That's a very strong commitment. Why don't you tell him, Rose?"

Rose avoided Carl's gaze and didn't speak.

Carrin pursed her lips before standing and starting slowly for the door. "Very well, then. We'll talk again in the future." Turning to Carl, she warned, "We will not resolve this matter in a court of law, but in the court of life. There is no way to avoid honoring your arrangement. You'll wish you had heard me out."

Carl closed the front door heavily behind their departing visitor. He turned to Rose. "I told you they would come back and to simply deny that they were real would do no good. Now, what are we going to do?"

Rose sat on the couch sobbing softly. "I don't know, Carl. I know we're eventually going to have to deal with it."

Carl shook his head. "I don't think what she was talking about is real. There's no such thing. It's got to be some kind of ploy."

"How did she know about our prayers? I didn't say anything to anyone. Did you?"

"No. Don't worry, they're not going to hurt Timmy in any way. I'll see to that."

CHAPTER FOUR

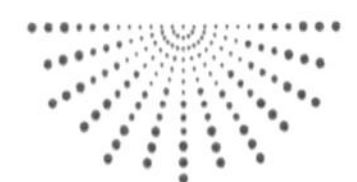

The doorbell rang just after supper. Timmy was next door at his friend's house, playing. When Carl opened the front door, a tall, good-looking woman waited on the other side. Carrin was back. With her was a stocky, gruff-looking gentleman who handed Rose a business card from Fargutt University. Like Carrin, it read that he was a Director of Inter-dimensional Studies at the university.

"Weston Phillips," he said, reaching to shake Carl's hand and then Rose's. Both of them ignored his offer. "May we speak with you for a few minutes?"

"No, you may not," Carl yelled. "You can get off my property before I call the cops."

Mr. Phillips looked at Carrin. She shook her head slowly.

"Do they not understand what lies ahead?" he wondered aloud.

The head shake became more definite. "No. They

don't. They wouldn't let me explain it to them. This is the same way they treated me last time."

"Well, I guess we all have to do what we have to do," he sighed. When he turned back to address Carl, the front door had been closed.

Inside the house, Carl peered into the eyepiece that allowed them to screen the visitors who came to their home. When he looked through it, he quickly snapped back and pulled the door open.

"Where'd they go?" he muttered.

Only a few seconds had passed. There was no possible way they could have walked to the end of the approach and driven away. Carl turned to look at Rose.

"D-di-did you see that?" he stuttered.

"See what?" Rose responded.

"They're gone. They were standing right there and now they're gone. Did you see them leave?"

Rose shook her head. "No, I didn't, but I wasn't watching either. Where do you think they went?"

Carl shook his head. "I don't know, but I do know they didn't drive away."

"Well, whatever. They're gone, and at least we don't have to deal with them for a while," Rose proclaimed.

"They'll be back," Carl remarked. "They'll keep coming back until we do as they say. You know that, don't you?"

Carl and Rose shared an eye-to-eye stare for a moment as tears welled in her eyes.

"No one is going to hurt Timmy. I promise," Carl reassured her.

Rose looked at him pleadingly. "What are we going to do?"

Carl shook his head. "I don't know. Maybe we should call the cops."

"And tell them what?" Rose demanded.

Again, Carl shook his head. "I don't know. We can't just sit here and wait for them to come back. If we don't do something now, we may not be able to in the future." Carl's voice trailed off at the end of his thought.

"Dad?"

Carl and Rose both turned to the small voice coming from the kitchen doorway. They glanced at each other for a moment and then Carl answered. "Yes, son."

"Was Mr. Phillips and Ms. Atworthy here again?"

"What does that matter? We think they're nothing but trouble. We're afraid that they want to hurt you or take you from us."

Timmy stated in a mature tone. "They're not here for that. Mom, remember when you told me I had a gift? Well, I do, and this is it."

Carl was unmoved. "I don't trust people like that, son. I'm thinking I should call the cops and have them questioned."

"Why are you afraid of Mr. Phillips and Ms. Atworthy?"

Again, his parents shared a glance.

"Because, son," Carl began, "as I said, we don't want them to hurt you."

Timmy replied quickly. "Oh, Dad, I just have a job to do, because of my gift. You know why they came. It's time."

"What do you mean?" Rose questioned.

Timmy walked into the living room and sat down on the couch, scooting his way back into the seat.

"Mom, Dad, can you guys sit down, please?"

Rose and Carl took seats in the standard chairs opposite the couch.

"Do you remember when I used to be scared at night?"

Both parents nodded.

"Well, it was Carrin and Wes trying to prepare me for this stage in my life. When they first contacted me, I acted like any other kid would. I freaked out. Then, last Thanksgiving when we stayed at the hotel near Grandma's house, they came in my dreams and took me on a little trip back to the spirit world. Then I remembered why I came here. There's nothing for any of us to be fearful of. I'm simply helping where I'm needed."

Timmy took a deep breath and sighed. Seeing the rapt attention in his parents' eyes, he continued, "You see, you really did make a promise. I was there. I heard it." Timmy paused for a moment and let his statement sink in. "You were not destined to have any children, yet your spirit guides saw the depth of your love and asked me if I would want to be part of your family. I jumped at the chance. I love you both and I know you love me, but any time there is a consideration offered, there is a price to be paid. It's not something you have to do. It's something I have to do. If I had told them I didn't want to be part of the family, none of this would be happening."

Rose sighed. "I wish it weren't happening right now."

He exclaimed, "Oh, Mom, don't be so dramatic! It's all going to be okay. When you hear what my responsibility is, you'll think it's wonderful."

Carl and Rose stared at each other. Was it possible this was their son talking? He sounded much older than eleven.

"What is it they want you to do?" Rose inquired, a tremor noticeable in her voice.

Timmy looked toward the front door. "I think it will be easier if they tell you."

Carl stood and walked to the entrance, pulling it open. Carrin and Wes stood waiting on the other side.

"May we come in?" Wes asked.

Without saying a word, Carl allowed the guests to enter. They sat on the small loveseat at the end of the room.

Timmy began. "Mom, Dad, Carrin and Wes are my mentors and were with me for a very long time in the spirit realms before I decided to come into this world. They are my friends and spirit guides. They're here to help me, help others."

Carl gave a little chuckle. "Help others? How are you going to help anyone? You're just a kid."

"Eleven *Earth* years, Carl," Carrin declared. "In the spirit realms, Tim is an ancient one. He has been helping others for several of your millennia. This is his finest hour."

Carl glanced at Rose. "What the hell do you mean, his finest hour? And what are spirit realms?"

Both of the visitors looked at Tim.

Wes urged, "Do you want to tell them?"

The young boy blinked, then nodded. "Okay." He then took a long, deep breath and slowly exhaled. "Mom, Dad, I know this is hard to believe, but if you hear me out, you'll understand why I need to do this. It's only for a short time and when I'm done, we can get on with being a family." Timmy glanced eye-to-eye with both of his parents. "I'm looking very much forward to that."

The explanation took considerably longer than any of them had expected. Despite their open mindedness, the concepts of a spiritual existence which actually paralleled the physical world were hard for Rose and Carl to accept. Their beliefs were much more traditional. Even though they believed there were spirits that could be reached from the physical world, the concepts of Heaven and Hell were still very strong for them. Timmy was about to give up and hand the reins back to the older guests when the phone rang.

After saying hello, Rose slowly sat down in the over-stuffed chair. During the next few minutes, she listened in silence, as everyone waited patiently. Finally, Rose said, "I understand, Momma … I love you, too." Then ended the call.

"Who was that?" Carl demanded.

Rose was as white as a sheet. She sat staring out into space, her eyes almost in tears.

"It was Momma."

Carl sat up. "Momma, who?"

Rose unfixed her gaze and turned to look at Carl. "My momma. She told me that what they're telling us is the truth and that we should listen to them."

Carl stood up. "Your momma? Your mother's dead."

Rose smiled slightly. "Yes, I know, but it was her. She told me something that only she and I knew. It couldn't have been anyone else."

Carl turned and glared at the others in the room. "Dead people don't call on the phone," he shouted. "It's a trick. They're trying to scam us."

The last part of his statement was drowned out by the ringing of the phone. Carl turned to look at it.

"I think that's for you, Carl," Rose indicated.

He answered reluctantly, "Hello!"

Carl began to shake noticeably. He nodded several times, swallowing deeply as he did, and then sat on the arm of the same chair which Rose still occupied. Like her, he listened for a few minutes and then offered, "I miss you, too … Right … Okay … I understand." Then he calmly hung up.

With that completed, he looked at the others and whispered, "I'm sorry. When do we begin?"

The call from Carl's boyhood friend, Ryan Cassar, convinced him that what was being offered was not a trick, but reality. Ryan had died in a boating accident when they were both sixteen years old. The day before, they'd snuck into Ryan's father's liquor cabinet, pilfered some whiskey, drank it, and ended up inebriated and sleeping in a tent in Ryan's back yard. Only he and Ryan knew that.

Rose's mother had recounted to her the events of Rose's first kiss, complete with dates, names, and places. There was no way that the information in her call could have been a trick.

Wes surveyed the surprised faces, smiled, and exclaimed, "Good. Now that we're all on the same page, we can begin. Timmy, are you ready?"

He nodded. "Yes, I am."

CHAPTER FIVE

Timmy felt the need to fill in the details of what lay ahead for him. Certainly, it would be better to operate with his parents in full understanding of what his responsibilities would be. Even though he spoke slowly and thoughtfully, his explanation of the duties which they had assigned him was difficult for Carl and Rose to accept.

Before Timmy was born into the physical world, he'd made an agreement with his spiritual teachers. Once he was old enough to carry out the missions, he would enter the void between the physical and spiritual worlds and help those who were lost or stranded in the ethers while attempting to reach the afterlife.

The system was really quite simple. The physical and spiritual worlds are connected by a tunnel of light. When a person's physical life ends at death, it's necessary that their spirit pass through this tunnel of light in order to reach their spiritual home. At the other end of the light, friends and family members who have preceded them in death wait to be reunited.

Most spirits find their way into the light easily. Unfortunately, some are unprepared for their physical death and are lost in the void while trying to find the light. This can happen because of an unanticipated death, unfinished business, or a lack of belief in the afterlife. These spirits wander in the ethers between the two worlds until a rescuer arrives to guide them into the tunnel of light leading to their spiritual haven. This rescue effort is the task Timmy had accepted.

The television flashed images on an unwatched screen. Timmy moved from his normal seat atop the ottoman into the large overstuffed chair which his father usually occupied. Sitting with his hands resting softly in his lap, he slowly closed his eyes and as he did, he disappeared from the view of the others.

Rose gasped. "Where did he go?"

Wes explained, "Relax, Rose. He'll be back soon enough. He's helping someone find their way home. Why don't you get something to eat and watch TV for a while?"

"Watch TV?" Carl yelled. "How the hell are we supposed to watch TV when our son is off doing your biddings?"

Wes wagged his finger in front of Carl. "Not our biddings, Carl, *your* biddings. Remember, you and Rose asked for the agreement. Tim just accepted the responsibility of carrying out your end of the bargain. Seriously, you worry too much. He'll be fine and back soon enough. Like I told you, just relax."

Carl got up and walked into the kitchen. They could hear him opening and slamming cupboard doors.

Rose hadn't said a word since Timmy vanished. She sat quietly in her chair, staring straight ahead. She had set herself into a state of numbness, simply waiting out the time until he returned.

Carl left the kitchen and went into the bedroom at the rear of the house. He was angry, frustrated, and afraid. He was also uncertain how well he could control his emotions. Rather than sit with their visitors, he felt it would be best if he kept his distance from the others.

"Mom, I'm hungry."

Rose's eyes opened and her head snapped up to see Timmy sitting in his original position in the center of his father's chair. She leaped to her feet and moved quickly to where he sat, sweeping him off the chair and into her arms.

"Oh, Timmy, I was so worried."

He looked over her shoulder to see his father stride into the room.

"Are you okay, son? You're not hurt, are you?"

Timmy threw back his head and laughed. "No, Dad, I'm not hurt. I'm fine. I'm just hungry, that's all. Can I have something to eat?"

"Of course," Rose answered, walking into the kitchen. "You can have anything you want."

A brief discussion ensued and soon Timmy was eating a hot dog with all the trimmings and potato chips.

Back in the living room, Carl turned to Wes. "So, it's done now, right?"

Wes scoffed. "Done? No, it's not done. We've only just

begun." Wes paused, looking into Carl's eyes. Seeing the concern there, he took a deep breath and sighed, softening his demeanor. "Carl, this is not a onetime project, it's ongoing. Truly, we have no idea how long it will last. That isn't our department. I will tell you that from experience, it will become a regular occurrence in your household. Please try to get used to it. Tim's not in any danger."

Carl stared eye-to-eye with the shorter man. After a moment's reflection, he slowly shook his head and pressed the issue, "How can you do this? What gives you the right?"

Wes extended his hands palms up and shrugged his shoulders. "We don't make the rules, we just carry them out. In the words of a familiar saying, 'I don't own the ship, I just steer it where they tell me to go.' Carrin is the same way. If you've got a problem with the arrangements, you'll have to talk to someone else. We can't help you."

"Wes is right," Carrin interjected. "We understand your fears, but there is really nothing to be afraid of. You'll see what we mean. Until he's called to do his work, he'll be every bit the eleven-year-old boy that you love. When it's time for him to help, he'll have the maturity necessary to complete his tasks."

"Tasks?" Carl snarled. "Who is this someone else? I want to talk to them."

"Dad. Please don't," Timmy pleaded. "I'm okay. This is what I want to do."

The three adults turned to see the small boy standing in the kitchen doorway. A trace of ketchup remained just outside his mouth on his cheek. He took several steps into the living room before Rose caught up with him from behind and wiped his mouth clean.

"Don't you see?" he continued, "someone has to do this. If I have a choice, I want to be the one. The fact that you and Mom made the agreement only made it possible. Today, I helped a nine-year-old boy find his parents on the other side. They had all passed years ago in a fire. Now, they're all happy again. Don't you want me to make people happy?"

Carl looked at Rose as he answered, "Yes, son. We'd like for you to make people happy. We just think you should wait a few years and enjoy your childhood for a while. When you're an adult, you can decide what you want to do with your life."

Timmy responded, "Dad, I've been an adult longer than you can imagine. This is what I want to do and I'm fully qualified and capable of doing it now. Please trust me on this. I'll have all the time I need to be your son and do family things. I promise."

Carrin and Wes stood, preparing to leave.

"I think Tim can answer any other questions that may remain," Carrin offered. "If you're still troubled or if there are lingering questions, just call us. We'll come and help if we can."

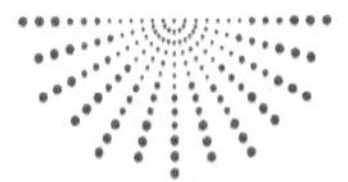

CHAPTER SIX

Timmy's life of travel and service became routine. No matter where he was, or what he was doing, day or night, he was subject to being called. Once, while he and his parents were at a restaurant having dinner with friends, Timmy excused himself on the premise of going to the restroom only to return several minutes later, as though nothing unusual had happened. He'd spent the time away helping a frightened mother find the tunnel and her children at the end of the light.

Time passed quickly, with more and more trips taking place each week. Timmy's work had become a significant part of their lives, and Carl and Rose had grown accustomed to his frequent absences. They formed every part of their lives around the necessity of him being available for his responsibilities.

At dinner one winter night, Carl raised a question. "Son, how long do you think this is going to continue?"

Timmy, now thirteen years old, looked up from his pork chops. He chewed thoughtfully for a moment and then shook his head.

"I don't know, Dad." He shrugged. "I really enjoy my calling. There are so many people that need help. Someone has to do it and I'm truly happy that it's me."

Rose looked at Carl and then at Timmy.

"Honey, it's been over two years. In the beginning, it was just once in a while. Now, it seems like every day–sometimes several times a day. We're just worried that you won't have a life to live if this keeps up."

Timmy remarked. "Mom, you worry too much. If I don't do this, who will?"

"Perhaps someone else who made a promise that they had to pay for," Carl suggested.

Timmy returned his father's stare. "Like, who?" he asked. "Do you mean, like you or mom?"

Carl shrugged. "Why not? You seem to like it. Why wouldn't we?"

"I really do like it, Dad. It's so important. Now that I have a lot of experience, I can help people all over the place, ones that others can't find. If you could be there just once ..." Timmy's voice trailed off as his mind wandered to memories of some of his rescues. "I really can't describe it. You'd have to be there." He slowly shook his head and swallowed his emotions. "You just have to be there to understand," he whispered again with finality.

"That's what we're talking about," Rose confirmed. "We want to help, too."

Timmy's face lit up. "You guys are the greatest, I mean that. But ..." he paused, "I don't know. It's never been done. I'm not sure it's allowed. It may not even be possible." His voice faded as he raised several unanswered questions in his mind.

Carl knew this was not the time to press the issue. Timmy was totally committed to helping others, and it brought deep emotions for him and those he helped. There would be more discussions soon. At least for now, the seed had been planted.

The ringing of the doorbell startled everyone. Rose looked at Carl.

"I wonder who that could be," she groaned, scooting her chair back from the table and rising to answer the door.

"Probably the neighbor," Carl guessed. "Checking to see if we've seen his cat." As Rose left the room, Carl pointed his fork at Timmy. "It's too bad you don't get paid for what you do."

"Oh, yes I do," he said with conviction. "Being able to live one day with you and Mom is better pay than any money could ever bring. It's worth it to me."

Carl was about to pat him on the back when Rose returned.

"Carl, we have company."

"Who's here?" he blurted without looking.

"It's Wes and Carrin."

Carl looked over at his son and slowly set his fork down. Pushing his chair away from the table and standing up, he muttered under this breath, "Now, what the hell do they want?" Carl walked into the living room to see their visitors standing in the center of the room. The animosities that existed over the years had faded into an attitude of tolerance. Still, Carl had never grown to appreciate Carrin or Wes.

"What can we do for you?" Carl grumbled, shaking hands with each of them.

The stocky man grinned a knowing smile in return as he released Carl's hand. "We're glad you asked," he began. "We are actually here for you and Rose."

Carl sighed deeply and looked at Rose before turning back to Wes and answering. "Okay. So, now what?"

Carrin smiled. "Carl, must you be so rude? This is an opportunity of a lifetime. Tim suggested we reward you both for your willingness to let him continue his duties."

Carl scoffed, grunting under his breath, staring into the eyes of the slender woman.

"Who said we were willing to let it continue? Matter of fact, we were just talking about how much longer you were planning on disrupting our lives."

Carrin's smile never wavered, nor did her stare into Carl's eyes. "Carl, we know what you've been talking about. Tim doesn't think the missions disrupt his life. Also, I think if you questioned Rose, and she told you the truth, she's secretly happy that he was selected for the position and she's proud of how well he's doing."

Carl agreed, "You may be right, but what if they're both bewitched?"

Carrin burst out laughing. "You don't honestly believe that any more than we do. Why don't you just lighten up a bit and accept that you've been given what we might call a very unique opportunity."

Carl rolled his eyes in disgust. A brief smile showed at

the corners of his mouth. "It's a golden ticket because you say it is, right?"

Timmy jumped in. "No, Dad. It really is rewarding. You may not know it yet, but when you hear what they have to offer, you'll wonder why you and Mom are so fortunate."

Rose smiled weakly, nervously turning her wedding ring on her finger. "Why don't we hear what they have to say, Carl? It might be something special."

Carl chuckled, then burst into a roar. "Special, is it? So, you're in cahoots with them on this?" He stared in mock disbelief at Rose, shook his head, then spouted, "You're all misguided. Whatever it is, I don't want any part of it. Count me out. I'm not interested."

The tension in the room cracked silently for several moments before Wes spoke up. "Carl, we overheard your discussions. Can we drop the facade and get down to business?"

Carl's face became sheepish. "What do you mean, you overheard our discussions? How could you do that?"

"All knowledge exists in the spirit realms," Carrin noted. "Like it or not, we know every thought that you have. We respect your desire to be in control, but it doesn't fit here. Also, we're not your enemies. Being angry or hard with us accomplishes nothing. When we get to the bottom line, your attitude, or your opinion of us, doesn't matter. Why not listen to what Wes has to say before you jump to conclusions? I believe your exact words were, 'Perhaps someone else who made a promise that they had to pay for.' Isn't that correct?"

Rose and Carl exchanged a look before Timmy begged, "Please, Dad? Won't you at least listen?"

Carl looked at his son. His eyes pleaded for acceptance. "Very well, then. What do you want to talk about?"

"Please sit down," Carrin began. When everyone was seated, she continued, "As Wes said, we are very pleased with Tim's efforts. In any other situation, we would consider his obligation, and yours, as fulfilled. However, he has asked to continue his service and we have accepted his request."

The look on Timmy's face confirmed that Wes and Carrin were acting on his wishes.

Carl turned back to look at Carrin. "So?"

"So," Carrin continued, "he has also requested that you and Rose be given an opportunity to join him in the efforts. He realizes, as do we, that there aren't enough qualified people available to do the task. He feels that you two have what it takes."

Carl sat up quickly, glancing in his son's direction. "Did you tell her what we were talking about?"

"I didn't have to, Dad. They heard you guys talking and came to you. I didn't say anything."

Rose cleared her throat. "Carl, I think maybe I do have what it takes. Can't we just try it and see what it's like? It may be something we can all do together ..." Rose's voice trailed off into silence. After a moment, she continued, almost whispering, "I've always wanted to do something special and worthwhile. When we first started seeing each other, you did too. Maybe this is what we always dreamed of."

Carl's stern outer demeanor often disguised the fact

that he loved Rose and Timmy very much. They were his Achilles' heel. He let his gaze move from one to the other. She was right. When he was younger, he had been very idealistic. He'd wanted to save the world with some heroic effort that made her proud of him. Now, years later, that opportunity lay waiting to be accepted. A chill ran through Carl's body. Timmy smiled weakly, "Please, Dad?"

Carl took a deep breath and slowly exhaled. He remembered the long discussions which he and Rose shared, outlining how they would change the world if they could. Where had all those visions of grandeur gone? Too much work and worry about money.

For the first time in a long while, he let his mind wander to the possibilities of what might be. If everything were as wonderful as everyone said, maybe this really was a unique opportunity. He certainly didn't want to let it slip away.

Carl stipulated, "Very well, then, I'll give it a try. But, if I want out, I'm out. Agreed?"

Everyone nodded in unison, "Agreed."

CHAPTER SEVEN

The first step that Rose and Carl took was to accompany Timmy on a rescue effort for a young man who had been killed in Vietnam. He was the radio operator on a helicopter which had been shot down. After gunfire hit the chopper, a flame in the aircraft blinded him for a few remaining moments before the crash. When death arrived and his spirit separated from his physical body, he was not aware that he could see again. He had been wandering in the ethers since 1969.

"Sergeant? Sergeant Kansik?" Timmy called. "Can you hear me?"

Quietly, Timmy, Rose, and Carl moved through the darkness, listening for any telltale signs that someone was nearby. They heard nothing.

"How long do we keep looking?" Carl asked.

"Sh-h-h-h-h," Timmy scolded in a whisper, "We continue calling until we find him. Sergeant Fred Kansik? Please say something."

"Is that you, Captain?" the faint voice responded.

"No, it isn't," Timmy replied. When they had finally reached the place where the young Marine stood, Timmy offered, "We're friends. We've come to help you."

"Thank God," the clean-cut young man declared. "I've been hurt and I can't see. Can you get me to the medics?"

"Don't worry, you can see. Simply allow your eyes to believe that you're no longer blind."

The sergeant slowly opened his eyes. He stammered, "I don't understand."

Timmy was in his element. Here, he was no longer simply a young boy. He was a guide, and today he was going to lead this brave soldier home.

Timmy's voice was calm. "Fred, you were in a fatal accident. Your physical life is over. Now it's time for you to move on. Since your passing, your mother, father, and even your brother have reached the spiritual afterlife. They'll be waiting for you when you go through the light to join them."

"Why doesn't it hurt?" Fred wanted to know.

Timmy reassured him, "Good things don't hurt. Just come with us. We're going to help you find your way to the other side."

The young hero looked around at his surroundings. "Why couldn't I have found it sooner?"

"You weren't ready before. You were in a state of shock from the accident."

They all walked a short distance to the opening of the light tunnel. From the outside, it appeared to be nothing more than a bright ring of brilliant white light pitched against total darkness. It looked more like an energy vortex than a tunnel. Rose and Carl peered into the entrance. To their surprise, the light extended far out into the distance. At the other end of the light, they saw Fred's mother and father anxiously awaiting his arrival. Tears welled in both their eyes.

Fred shared a parting glance with his rescuers. "They really are there," he whispered, with disbelief in his voice, then louder added, "I'm going home."

He turned and quickly shook everyone's hand. "Thank you. Thank you all very much," he exclaimed.

The emotions of the moment rendered Carl, Rose, and Timmy speechless. They all simply waved as Fred gave a final salute, turned, and disappeared into the brilliance of the light.

"Time to go," Timmy said.

As quickly as they had left the comfort of their living room, they were all back in their favorite chairs.

The game show emcee was droning on about how much money the contestant had won. The Bakers sat in quiet reflection.

"Is it always like that?" Carl finally asked.

Timmy shook his head. "No, Dad. This was an easy one. Sometimes you look for what seems like days without success. Eventually, you'll find who you're looking for. Your instincts will lead you to them."

Carl rephrased his question. "I meant, are they all so emotional? I've never felt anything like that before."

Timmy confided, "Wait until you have to find a young child. That's when the emotions are strongest."

"Everyone's someone's young child," Rose added softly, staring into the distance. "Do the emotions ever go away?"

"No, Mom. The fear and anguish go away, but the deep feeling of joy never subsides. Think of what Fred and his family are talking about right now. You don't think there's any sorrow there, do you?"

"You were right, son. I was mistaken. I've been wrong about a lot of things in life. Maybe this is my chance to make things right. When do we go again?"

Timmy smiled. "Now, you're talking. They'll come to us when it's time. It's no harder than listening to your inner voice tell you where to look. You'll actually feel it when you get close to the person you're looking for. Once you get there, just call their name. They'll find you. Everyone wants to go home. Even when they're not actively thinking about it, they want to cross over. All we do is offer the road map."

Timmy tilted his head away from his father's searching face to look at the now empty chair where his mother had just been sitting. "See, Dad? Even Mom was ready to help. There's so much work to do. We're all needed. When you see how wonderful it is to help someone on your own, you'll know this is what you were brought into the universe to do. I promise, it will absolutely blow your mind with happiness."

Carl smiled softly. "I sure hope you're right, son. I would look forward to that."

The game show had just broken to commercial when Carl sensed the lights around him dimming. In only a moment, he was transported into a veil of total darkness. *Odd*, he thought. *I can't see, but I know where I'm going.* He felt the fears of a young girl pulling at his heart. Carl focused his attention on the black abyss that had surrounded him and to the energy which seemed to call him by name. It was his first solo effort. Timmy was right. His destiny would be more glorious than he ever dreamed!

"Lily," he called softly into the darkness. "Lily, can you hear me?"

~

Thank you for reading *The Promise*.
If you enjoyed this story, the best way to let other readers know, is to post a review.

If you want to continue The Starlite Supernatural Mystery Series, our standalone shorts can be read in any order.

Find them at your favorite retailer
https://books2read.com/MicheleFraser

BOOKS 2 READ

For Additional Options
linktr.ee/RayandMicheleFraser

AUTHOR NOTES

Receive an exciting look into *Mary* by signing up for our newsletter using the Bookfunnel link below.

https://dl.bookfunnel.com/xpkhinq30n

Plus, get behind the scenes tidbits and learn about new releases.

Mary
A young girl with a mysterious background
triggers a shocking search into
the dark reaches of time.

Reviews

Mary

"A short paranormal novella that's just about ninety pages long: I enjoyed every aspect of it. I wished it was longer, but just because I loved the writing style - the characters. The flow of the book was just perfection. Also, I liked the action part at the beginning and the mystery each chapter brought. It never had a dull moment."
- Midnightstorybook

Mary

"Read it as an ARC. Absolutely loved this story. Held my attention the whole time. The plot was consistent from beginning to end. Gave off a murder mystery vibe without murder. No cliffhangers with a great unexpected ending. Suspenseful and mysterious. Definitely worth reading if you want to try out the supernatural mystery genre."
- Elizabeth S.

Mary

"Every time I thought I had an idea of who Mary was and where she came from, I'd learn about new piece of the puzzle and have to throw all my theories out the window. Things get stranger as the story progresses, which just made me more eager to figure out what was really going on. I felt a bit bad for our main character Jason and his quest to return Mary to her family, but I admired how determined he was to help such an odd little girl.

For such a brief story, "Mary" is packed full of intrigue and mystery - who is this little girl, where is she from, and why doesn't she understand how to drink a milkshake? I can guarantee you won't see the answer coming!

I really enjoyed this read, and I'd recommend it to anyone looking for a novella that will keep them guessing. I'm looking forward to reading more by Ray and Michele Fraser - thank you so much to the authors for the opportunity to read this book!"
- Anna

Check out our other unique spellbinding shorts.
They're the perfect escape when
you're pressed for time.

The Starlite Supernatural Mystery Series

Haunted

The Wind

The Promise

Mary

1421 Maple

Coming Soon

Enter the web of intrigue, suspense, and danger in

The Sean Thomas Paranormal Mystery Series

Book 1 - *A Switch in Time*

For a complete list of Ray and Michele's books

or

to request signed paperbacks visit their website.

www.rayandmichelefraser.com

Find them at your favorite retailer

https://books2read.com/MicheleFraser

BOOKS 2 READ

For Additional Options

linktr.ee/RayandMicheleFraser

ABOUT THE AUTHORS

Ray and Michele are a full-time writing team with a serious passion for storytelling. They combine their love of writing, vivid imagination, and years of experience as professional spirit mediums to guide their readers into uncharted territories.

In 1994, Ray's intuitions fostered by Cherokee and Scottish ancestry, led him to open Mystiques-West Metaphysical Center in Michigan. During the twenty-three years of operation, Ray hosted a #1 radio talk show and a live TV show, called "The Mystical Connection." They performed home cleansing, organized ghost hunts, taught classes in mediumship, and led weekly public seances to connect clients to their departed loved ones on the other side. The messages from spirit have helped many to find peace. Ray also facilitated the last four National Houdini Seances sponsored by Houdini historian Sid Radner.

In addition to readings and life coaching sessions, Ray's work as an ordained minister has provided his clientele with years of grief and relationship counseling, weddings, and funerals.

As a screenwriter, Michele brings her love of film into the fold by incorporating her own style of creativity into their endeavors. She's also the backbone of the editing process, social media management, cover design, and marketing.

Ray and Michele infuse their stories with mystery, intrigue, tales of the afterlife, and other worldly phenomena to create a fascinating and adventurous journey for readers.

www.rayandmichelefraser.com

Ray's extensive background and keen storytelling abilities combined with Michele's love of screenwriting and editing has made them a powerhouse duo.

For more info
linktr.ee/RayandMicheleFraser

… a cozy thriller?! That sounded right up my alley!

I've never experienced winter in New Hampshire, but I spent several winters growing up in ND & MN so I knew just how cold and hopeless Mike felt as he raced through the storm.

This short story was a quick & easy read, but it still had plenty of suspense to keep me hooked, wondering how it would all play out. The ending was great!!

I'm looking forward to getting my hands on more stories by this great pair!

Many thanks to the authors for an ARC of this short story in exchange for a review."
- Katie & Roland

Haunted
"Ray and Michele do not disappoint. I could not put this book down. It left me wanting to know more. I'm a big fan of haunted houses and was very intrigued with this story. I honestly didn't see the story going the way it did. I actually felt as if I was there. I felt all the emotions the characters felt. I'm still in awe at the story and cannot wait until their next book!!"
- Shana L.

Haunted
"A perfectly paranormal novella for this spooky season! Haunted was a quick and captivating read. I loved the

story of this haunted house and the mystery of finding out what happened to the spirit tormenting its current owners. I was drawn to reading about Brett and his journey to learning how to communicate and help spirits who haven't passed on to the other side. The Fraser's once again do a great job creating characters and settings that you can really get connect with in the time it takes to finish the story. This was an easy 5 star read for me. I loved this fast, fun read and look forward to the next of the Starlite Mysteries!"
- Mia

Mary

"I went into this novella only knowing that it was described as a paranormal mystery. I love paranormal books but I don't read mystery too often so I was interested to see how these two genres combined. Immediately as the story began I was interested in discovering who exactly this mysterious Mary was. I thought I had an idea as to where things were going and who Mary was but I was so wrong! I don't want to spoil anything, but when Jason started digging up the past I certainly didn't expect the story to go where it did. This was a quick yet captivating read that I'd recommend if you're a fan of either paranormal or mystery."
- MissS3LFD3STRUKT

Mary

"Fun mystery involving action, the occult and a dark past. Jason Arnold is on a plane about to land when it crashes to the ground. As he races to escape the fiery wreckage, he spots a little girl trapped and alone. He rescues her and they both make it to safety.

And then the mystery begins. Where are her parents? Who is this little girl?

When he finds out her name is Mary Parker, the mystery only deepens. There is no record of a Mary Parker being a passenger or ever even boarding the plane. How did she get there? Jason finds himself driven to find out who she is and where she came from. He feels responsible -after all, he saved her. But perhaps some secrets are better left unexplored...

I really enjoyed this story. It went in a very different direction than I expected and felt very new and fresh."
- Deirdre H.

1421 Maple

"I really enjoyed this short story! It's one of those thrillers that you can finish on a lunch break and feel like you spent 45 minutes in an alternate universe. I was intrigued from the beginning, but a plot twist came around and I had to keep reading to see what was going on. Perfect for those just getting into a thriller genre!"
- Brenna P., Outreach Librarian

1421 Maple

"I loved this novella style story! I love paranormal reads! I wish it was a full length book, because I really enjoyed the storyline and would have loved to see more! I loved the relationship with Jimmy and his father, a strong loving relationship is few and far between in books! I felt Jimmy's feelings with the lot build, I've been there so it was very relatable. It had a great storyline from beginning to end, I loved the depiction of the new neighbors and the mystery of it all."
- Melynda D.

Sarah

"This is a page turner. Sarah finds herself in a destructive marriage that is not at all what she thought she was getting into. Charlie is charming on the outside with an evil heart. To survive, she had to do something drastic. But will she ever be truly free from her torturing husband? Fans of A Tell Tale Heart will find this an interesting twist on a classic story."
- Brook